The Usborne
FIRST
COOKBOOK

Angela Wilkes

Illustrated by Stephen Cartwright

Edited by Rebecca Gilpin and designed by Sally Griffin

Americanization by Carrie Armstrong   US expert: Barbara Tricinella

Contents

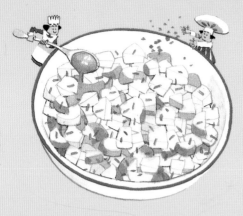

Before You Start

Ingredients

Before you begin, read these two pages. Then, read the recipe you are going to cook and make sure that you have everything you need. If you don't understand something, turn to pages 70-71, where you'll find explanations of cooking words, and pictures of things that you'll need.

At the beginning of each recipe, you'll find a list of all the ingredients you will need. Use measuring cups and spoons to measure ingredients. If you need to cut or slice any ingredients, do this before you start to cook.

Wipe mushrooms with a damp paper towel, then slice them.

Cut the ends off a clove of garlic and peel it before you crush it.

Slice or chop onions as finely as you can.

Don't start cooking unless there is an adult there to help you.

All of the recipes in this book are for four people, unless they say otherwise.

Your Oven

Cook things on the middle shelf of your oven unless the recipe says something different. If you need to move any of the shelves, do this before turning on your oven. Turn your oven on to the temperature given in the recipe so that it has heated up by the time you need to use it. If you have a fan oven, you will need to use a lower heat, so look in its instruction book to see how much lower the temperature needs to be.

Things To Remember

Be Careful

Be very careful when you use a sharp knife, and always cut on a cutting board. Put hot dishes onto a heatproof mat or wooden board, rather than straight onto a work surface or a table.

To avoid knocking saucepans over, always turn the handles to the side of your stove. Never leave the kitchen while electric or gas burners are on.

Always put on oven mitts before you pick up anything hot. Make sure you wear them when you're lifting things into or out of your oven.

Follow The Recipe

Don't be tempted to open the oven door while things are cooking unless the recipe tells you to, or you think something is burning.

Remember to turn off your oven when you've finished cooking.

Start Clean And Stay Clean

Always wash your hands before you start cooking and stay as clean as you can. Wear an apron and roll up your sleeves. If you spill anything, wipe it up right away.

Baked Tomatoes

Ingredients

- 4 large tomatoes
- salt and black pepper
- 4 eggs
- 1 Tablespoon chopped parsley

Use the biggest tomatoes you can find for this recipe. If you're very hungry, cook two tomatoes for each person.

Preheat your oven to 350°F.

1. Wipe a paper towel in a little margarine or butter. Use it to grease the insides of a shallow, ovenproof baking dish.

2. Slice off the top of each tomato and put the tops aside. Scoop out the insides with a spoon. Then, sprinkle a pinch of salt and pepper into each tomato.

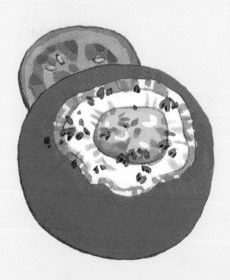

3. Put the tomatoes into the baking dish. Break an egg into each tomato and sprinkle them with a pinch of salt and some chopped parsley.

4. Put the tops back on the tomatoes. Bake them in the oven for about 20 minutes or until the eggs have set.

5. Eat the tomatoes right away, with crusty bread and butter.

Welsh Rarebit

Ingredients

- ¾ cup grated cheese
- 1 teaspoon mustard
- 1 egg, beaten
- 3 or 4 drops
    Worcestershire sauce
- salt and black pepper
- 4 slices of bread
- 2 tomatoes, sliced

1. Mix the cheese, mustard, egg, Worcestershire sauce and a pinch of salt and pepper together in a bowl.

2. Put the slices of bread in the broiler. Toast them on one side, then lift them out.

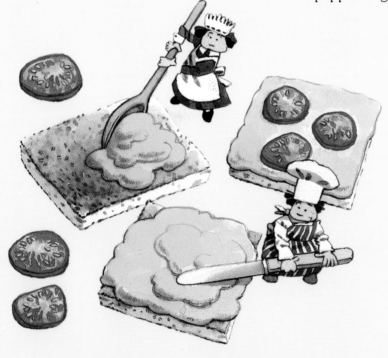

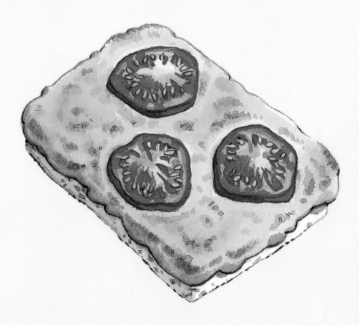

3. Spread the cheese mixture thickly over the untoasted sides of the bread, then lay a few slices of tomato on top.

4. Put the pieces of toast back under the grill and cook them until the cheese is light brown and bubbly.

Cream Cheese Dip

Ingredients

- ⅔ cup light cream
- 1½ cups (12 oz.) cream cheese
- 2 finely chopped green onions
- 2 Tablespoons chopped parsley
- 2 Tablespoons chopped chives
- 2 teaspoons chopped mint
- 1 clove garlic, crushed
- 1 teaspoon lemon juice
- salt and black pepper
- celery, carrot and cucumber, for dipping

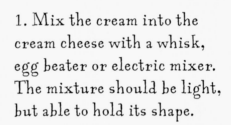

1. Mix the cream into the cream cheese with a whisk, egg beater or electric mixer. The mixture should be light, but able to hold its shape.

2. Mix in the chopped green onions, herbs, garlic and lemon juice. Stir in a pinch of salt and pepper, too.

3. Cut the ends off some celery sticks, then peel a few carrots and half a cucumber with a potato peeler. Cut them all into thin sticks.

4. Spoon the dip into a shallow bowl and add the vegetables. Use them to scoop up the dip to eat.

Garlic Bread

Ingredients

- 6 Tablespoons butter, softened
- 1 Tablespoon chopped parsley
- 1 Tablespoon chopped chives
- 2 cloves garlic, crushed
- 1 stick French bread

Preheat your oven to 400°F.

1. Mix the butter, herbs and garlic in a bowl with a wooden spoon.

2. Make lots of cuts along the loaf, but don't cut all the way through it.

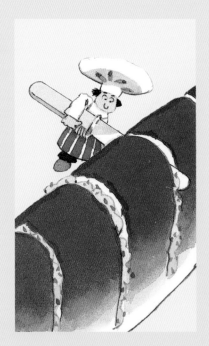

3. Using a knife, spread both sides of each cut with some of the butter mixture.

4. Wrap the loaf in foil. Put it in the oven and bake it for 10-15 minutes.

5. Eat the bread while it is hot. It tastes delicious with a salad.

Vegetable Soup

Ingredients

- ¾ lb. potatoes
- ¾ lb. tomatoes
- ¾ lb. leeks or onions
- 2 Tablespoons butter
- salt and black pepper
- 2½ cups water
- 2 teaspoons sugar
- 2 Tablespoons milk

1. Peel the potatoes with a potato peeler. Using a sharp knife, carefully slice them, then cut them into cubes.

2. Spoon the tomatoes into a container of boiling water. After a minute, lift them out again.

3. Peel the skin off the tomatoes with your fingers. Then, cut the peeled tomatoes into chunks with a knife.

4. Cut the tops and roots off the leeks or onions. Peel off the outer layer, then cut them in half lengthwise. Rinse them under cold running water until they are clean, then shake them dry. Cut them into thin slices.

5. Gently melt the butter in a big saucepan over low heat. Add the sliced leeks or onions, then cook them slowly until they are soft, stirring all the time.

6. Add the chopped tomatoes to the pan. Stir them in with a wooden spoon, then cook them slowly until they are soft. Add the potatoes, a pinch of salt and pepper, the water and the sugar. Put a lid on the pan and simmer the soup for about 25 minutes, until the potatoes are soft.

7. Take the soup off the heat and leave it to cool for 10 minutes. Then, get someone to help you to blend it in a blender to make it smooth.

8. Carefully pour the soup back into the pan. Taste it and add more pepper, if you like. Then, gently heat it over a low heat.

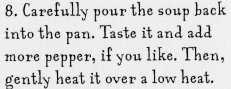

9. Stir the milk into the soup, then serve it.

Omelette

Ingredients

To make 1 omelette:

- 2 eggs
- salt and black pepper
- 1 Tablespoon butter
- a filling, if you like
  (see below)

Omelettes are very quick to make. You can make a plain omelette or add one of the fillings below.

This recipe uses two eggs, which will make an omelette for one person.

1. Break the eggs into a bowl, then add a pinch of salt and pepper. Beat the eggs lightly with a fork.

Try one of these tasty fillings, or think of one of your own. You only need to use a little filling in each omelette.

- a little grated cheese

- chopped tomato gently cooked in butter

- a Tablespoon of chopped parsley and chives

- sliced ham or cooked bacon, cut into pieces

2. Melt the butter in a small frying pan. Carefully swirl it around. When it foams, pour in the eggs.

3. When the omelette begins to set around the edges, sprinkle your filling over the top.

4. Gently pull the edges into the middle with a fork. Then, tilt the pan to let the runny egg flow to the sides to cook.

5. When the top of the omelette has set but still looks creamy, carefully loosen the edges with a palette knife. Fold the omelette over, then slide it onto a plate.

6. Eat the omelette right away, while it is hot. You could eat your omelette with salad and crusty bread.

French Toast

Ingredients

- 4 eggs
- salt and black pepper
- 4 Tablespoons butter
- 2 Tablespoons cooking oil
- 4 thick slices of white bread, with the crusts cut off

French toast is yummy, and it's very quick and easy to make. You can eat it by itself for breakfast or have it with a salad for supper.

BE CAREFUL

1. Break the eggs into a shallow dish. Beat them well, then mix in a pinch of salt and pepper.

2. Heat the butter and oil in a frying pan over medium heat for about a minute.

3. Dip the slices of bread into the egg, letting any extra egg drip back into the dish.

4. Fry the slices of bread on both sides, until they are golden brown and crisp. Lift them out with a spatula and eat them right away, while they are hot. Sprinkle them with sugar and cinnamon, if you like.

Twice Baked Potatoes

Ingredients

- 4 large potatoes, scrubbed clean with a brush
- 4 Tablespoons butter
- ½ cup chopped ham
- ¾ cup grated cheese
- 2 Tablespoons milk
- 1 Tablespoon chopped parsley
- salt and black pepper

Preheat your oven to 400°F.

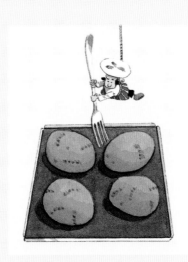

1. Put the potatoes onto a baking tray and prick them with a fork. Bake them for 45 minutes - 1 hour.

2. Carefully push a skewer into the biggest potato. If it is soft, it is cooked – if not, cook the potatoes for a little longer.

3. When the potatoes are cooked, cut them in half lengthways and scoop out the middles into a bowl.

4. Mash the potato with a fork. Then, mix in the rest of the ingredients. Add a pinch of salt and pepper.

5. Fill the potato skins with the mixture and bake them for another 15 minutes. Decorate them with parsley.

Deviled Eggs

Ingredients

- 4 eggs
- mayonnaise
- salt and black pepper
- finely chopped parsley
- a dash of paprika,
  if you like

Cooling the eggs quickly stops a black ring from forming around the yolks.

1. Put the eggs into a saucepan of cold water. Boil the water, then let it simmer for ten minutes.

2. Take the pan off the heat and put it under cold running water. Run cold water over the eggs until they are cool.

3. Tap the eggs on a hard surface, to crack the shells. Peel the shells off, then cut the eggs in half lengthways.

4. Using a teaspoon, scoop the yolks into a bowl. Mash them with a fork, then stir in some mayonnaise to make a thick paste.

5. Mix in a pinch of salt and pepper, then spoon the mixture into the hollows in the egg whites. Sprinkle chopped parsley over them.

Sausage Rolls

Ingredients

- pastry made from:
  - 6 Tablespoons butter
  - 1½ cups all-purpose flour
  - 3-5 Tablespoons cold
    water
  - a pinch of salt
- ½ lb. (8 oz.) sausage meat
- 1 egg, beaten

Preheat your oven to 435°F.
Grease a baking sheet, too (see page 71).

1. Make pastry, following the steps 1 and 2 on page 26. Roll it out into a rectangle about 6 inches wide, then cut it into two strips.

2. Cut the meat in half. Roll it into two 'sausages' that are as long as the pastry. Lay them on the middle of the pastry strips.

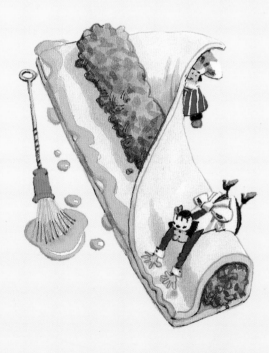

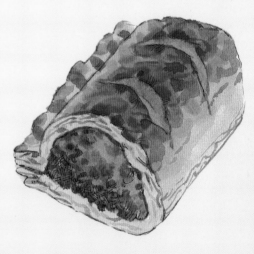

3. Brush the beaten egg along the sides of the pastry strips. Fold one side of each strip over the sausage meat and firmly press the edges together.

4. Cut the sausage rolls into chunks. Cut two slits in the top of each one, then brush them with beaten egg. Put them on a baking tray.

5. Bake the sausage rolls for 20-25 minutes, until they are golden brown. Carefully lift them out of the oven and eat them.

Easy Breaded Fish

Ingredients

- 2 eggs
- salt and black pepper
- 1 Tablespoon chopped parsley
- 1 Tablespoon chopped chives
- 4 Tablespoons breadcrumbs
- the grated rind of a small lemon
- 8 fillets of fish
- 1 Tablespoon cooking oil

1. Beat the eggs in a shallow dish. Mix in a pinch of salt and pepper. Then, mix the herbs, breadcrumbs and lemon rind together in another shallow dish.

2. Dry the fillets of fish on paper towels. Dip them into the egg, then into the breadcrumbs, until they are evenly coated all over.

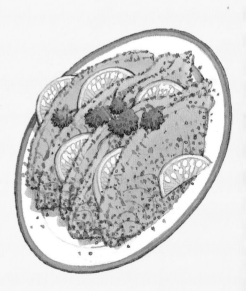

3. Heat the oil in a frying pan over medium heat. Fry the fillets for about three minutes on each side, or until they are golden brown.

4. Lift out the fillets of fish with a spatula. Lay them on paper towels, to drain off any excess oil.

5. You could serve the fish with wedges of lemon, boiled potatoes and a salad.

Cheesy Zucchini

Ingredients

- 2 lbs. zucchini
- 3 eggs
- 1 cup light cream
- salt and black pepper
- a pinch of nutmeg
- ¾ cup grated cheese

Preheat your oven to 400°F.
Grease a shallow ovenproof dish, too (see page 71).

1. Slice the zucchini, then cook them in boiling water for five minutes, then carefully drain them through a colander.

2. Beat the eggs and cream in a bowl. Add a pinch of salt and pepper, and the nutmeg.

Eat the zucchini by itself or as a vegetable with a main dish.

3. Spread the zucchini over the bottom of the dish. Pour the egg mixture evenly over them and sprinkle the grated cheese on top.

4. Bake the zucchini for about 20 minutes, until the egg mixture has set and the cheese is golden brown and bubbly.

Hamburgers

Ingredients

- 1 lb. ground beef
- 1 small onion, chopped
- 1 egg, beaten
- salt and black pepper
- 4 hamburger buns
- a little cooking oil

1. Mix the ground beef, onion, egg and a pinch of salt and pepper in a bowl. Cut the buns in half and toast the cut sides in the broiler or grill.

2. Divide the mixture into four pieces. Use your hands to make each piece into a flattened circle.

You could eat your burger with a baked potato and a salad, instead of on a bun.

3. Brush oil over the burgers. Grill them on high heat for 6-10 minutes on each side, then carefully lift them out.

4. Put each burger in a bun. Add slices of cheese, sliced tomatoes, lettuce leaves or mayonnaise, if you like.

Pork Chops With Apple

Ingredients

- about 3 small onions (1 lb.)
- about 3 medium cooking apples (1 lb.)
- salt and black pepper
- 1 Tablespoon sugar
- 4 pork chops
- butter

Preheat your oven to 350°F.

1. Peel and slice the onions and apples. Then, spread the onions over the bottom of a casserole dish.

2. Sprinkle a pinch of salt and pepper over the onions. Lay half of the apple slices on top, then sprinkle the sugar over them.

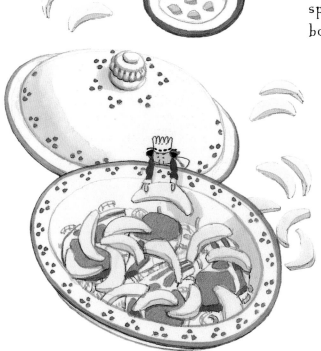

3. Lay the pork chops on top. Add a pinch of salt and pepper, then the rest of the apple. Add little pieces of butter on top, too.

4. Put the lid on the casserole dish, then bake the pork for 1-1½ hours, until it is tender. Serve it with potatoes and vegetables.

Cheese Soufflé

Ingredients

- 3 large eggs
- white sauce made from:
  - 1½ cups milk
  - 2 Tablespoons butter
  - ¼ cup all-purpose flour
- ¾ cup grated cheese
- a pinch of nutmeg
- salt and black pepper

Handy Tips

- Use eggs that are at room temperature, not chilled.

- Stop whisking the egg whites as soon as they stand up in peaks.

- You need to fold in the egg whites with a metal spoon (see page 71).

- A soufflé starts to sink as soon as you take it out of the oven, so you need to eat it right away.

A cheese soufflé looks amazing but is surprisingly easy to make. It's made with whisked egg white, which has a lot of air in it, and it puffs up as it cooks. Its name means 'puffed up' in French.

Before you turn your oven on, move one shelf to the middle and take out the shelves above it.

Preheat your oven to 375°F.
Grease a 1 quart soufflé dish or round ovenproof dish, too (see page 71).

1. Crack one egg at a time on the rim of a bowl. Carefully slide the yolk from one half of the shell to the other, being careful not to break the yolk.

2. As you slide the yolk around, the egg white will dribble into the bowl. Pour the yolk into another bowl. Beat all the yolks together.

3. Make a white sauce, following the steps on page 24. Then, stir in the cheese, nutmeg, egg yolks and a pinch of salt and pepper.

You can use an electric mixer, if you have one.

4. Whisk the egg whites until they form soft peaks when you lift the whisk or egg beater. Stir a Tablespoon of them into the sauce, then gradually fold in the rest. Don't beat the mixture, or the soufflé won't rise.

5. Pour the mixture into the greased dish and put it into the oven. Bake the soufflé for 30-35 minutes, until it is golden brown and puffy. Don't open the oven door while it is cooking. Serve it with a green salad.

Bacon And Potato Casserole

Ingredients

- 3 Tablespoons butter
- 4 Tablespoons all-purpose flour
- 1½ cups milk
- salt and black pepper
- 1 large onion
- 10 strips of bacon
- 4 large potatoes

Preheat your oven to 350°F.

1. To make a white sauce, melt the butter in a saucepan over low heat. Stir in the flour, a spoonful at a time. Let the mixture cook for a minute, then take it off the heat. Stir in the milk, a little at a time.

This page shows you how to make a white sauce. Once you've made it, put it aside. You'll be pouring it over the top of the casserole in step 7.

2. Put the pan back on the heat. As the sauce heats up it gets thicker, so keep stirring it to keep it from getting lumpy. When it boils, turn down the heat and simmer it until it is thick and creamy. Stir in a pinch of salt and pepper, then take the pan off the heat.

3. Peel the onions, then chop them finely with a sharp knife.

4. Carefully cut the bacon into small pieces.

5. Peel the potatoes with a potato peeler, then slice them.

6. Grease an ovenproof dish, then fill it with layers of potatoes, then onions, then bacon. Sprinkle a pinch of salt and pepper over each layer and finish with a layer of potatoes.

7. Pour the sauce over the top. Put the casserole on the middle shelf of your oven and bake it for about 1½ hours. Carefully move it to the top shelf for the last 20 minutes, to brown the top.

Quiche

Ingredients

- 6 Tablespoons butter
- 1½ cups all-purpose flour
- a pinch of salt
- 3-5 Tablespoons cold
  water

For the filling:
- 6 strips of bacon
- 2 large eggs
- 1 cup milk
- salt and black pepper
- a pinch of nutmeg

A quiche is a kind of French flan. The recipe for this creamy bacon quiche comes from an area called Lorraine in Eastern France.

Preheat your oven to 400°F. Grease an 8 inch pie pan, too.

1. Cut up the butter. Put it in a bowl with the flour and salt. Rub them with your fingertips until they look like breadcrumbs.

2. Sprinkle the water over the mixture in the bowl. Mix everything with your hands until you make a soft ball of dough that doesn't stick to the bowl.

If the dough is crumbly, add more water. If it is sticky, add more flour. Sprinkle flour over a clean work surface and on a rolling pin before you roll out the pastry.

3. Roll out the pastry with a rolling pin, until it is thin and almost round. Press it into the pan, prick it with a fork and trim off any edges.

4. Cut the bacon into small pieces, then fry it gently over low heat until it is crispy.

5. Beat the eggs and milk in a bowl, then add a pinch of salt, pepper and nutmeg.

6. Sprinkle the bacon over the pastry, then pour the egg mixture over the top.

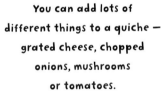

You can add lots of different things to a quiche — grated cheese, chopped onions, mushrooms or tomatoes.

7. Put the quiche in the oven and cook it for 30 minutes. It is ready when the egg mixture has set in the middle and is golden brown. Eat it hot with vegetables, or let it cool and eat it with a salad.

Spaghetti

Ingredients

- 1 clove garlic
- 2 onions
- 4 strips of bacon
- 1 Tablespoon cooking oil
- 1 lb. ground beef
- 16 oz. can chopped tomatoes
- 2 Tablespoons tomato paste
- a pinch of dried basil
- salt and black pepper
- 16 oz. package spaghetti

This spaghetti is made with a meat and tomato, or bolognese, sauce. The important thing to remember about spaghetti is not to overcook it – it should be soft but still have a little 'bite' to it.

1. Peel and crush the garlic. Peel and finely chop the onions. Then, cut the bacon into small pieces.

2. Heat the oil in a large frying pan over low heat. Gently fry the garlic and onion until they are soft. Add the bacon, and then the meat, to the pan. Break up the meat with a wooden spoon, then keep turning it and stirring it until it is brown all over.

3. Add the tomatoes, tomato paste, basil and a pinch of salt and pepper. Stir the mixture well, then put a lid on the pan and simmer it for 20 minutes.

4. While the sauce is cooking, heat a large saucepan of water. Add a pinch of salt and a teaspoon of cooking oil, to keep the spaghetti from sticking.

5. When the water is boiling, add the spaghetti. Push it gently into the pan – it will slide down as the ends begin to soften.

6. Cook the spaghetti for 8-10 minutes, until it is soft but not soggy. Drain it through a colander over your sink.

7. Put the spaghetti into a warm serving dish and pour the meat sauce over it. Mix them well.

8. Serve the spaghetti with grated cheese to sprinkle over it, and a green salad.

Cooking Rice

Ingredients

- 1 Tablespoon cooking oil
- 1 cup white long grain rice
- 2 cups boiling water
- a pinch of salt

Rice can be tricky to cook, but if you follow the package directions, you will have fluffy, perfectly cooked rice every time.

1. Heat the oil in a saucepan over low heat. Stir in the rice, then cook it for a few minutes, until it looks transparent.

2. Pour in the boiling water and add the salt. Put a lid on the pan and let the rice simmer. Don't stir it while it is cooking.

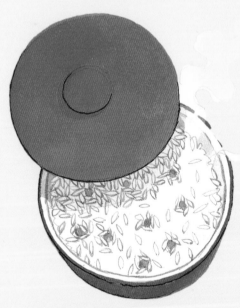

4. After 15 minutes, lift off the lid carefully. The rice should have absorbed all the water. If not, cook it for a little longer.

5. Bite a few grains to see if they are soft. If they are still hard, add a little more water and cook the rice for a little longer.

6. When the rice is cooked, spoon it into a warm serving dish. Fluff it up with the prongs of a fork.

Tasty rice

Ingredients

- 4 tomatoes
- 125g (4oz) mushrooms
- 2 onions
- 1 red pepper
- 6 rashers of bacon
- 2 tablespoons of cooking oil
- 125g (4oz) peas
- 2 tablespoons of tomato purée
- 225g (8oz) freshly cooked rice (see page opposite)

In this recipe, you make the sauce, then stir cooked rice into it. Cook the rice while the sauce is cooking in step 3.

1. Peel the tomatoes (see page 10), then chop them. Wipe the mushrooms on some kitchen paper, then slice them. Peel and chop the onions, too.

2. Cut the ends off the pepper. Cut it in half and remove the seeds, then cut it into slices. Cut the bacon into small pieces.

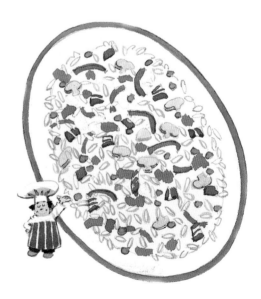

3. Heat the oil, onion and bacon in a large saucepan over a low heat. When the onion is soft, add the other vegetables and tomato purée. Stir them well, then put a lid on the pan. Cook the mixture for 15-20 minutes, stirring it often.

4. Mix the rice into the vegetable mixture. Heat the mixture over a medium heat until it is hot.

Lemon Chicken

Ingredients

- 4 Tablespoons honey
- 4 skinless boneless chicken breasts
- the juice of a large orange
- the juice of half a lemon
- 1 Tablespoon soy sauce
- salt and black pepper

Preheat your oven to 300°F.
Grease an ovenproof dish with butter, too.

1. Rub a Tablespoon of honey over each chicken breast, then lay them in the ovenproof dish. Wash your hands.

2. Mix the orange juice, lemon juice and soy sauce. Add a pinch of salt and pepper, then pour the mixture over the chicken.

5. Spoon the chicken onto plates and pour the sauce over it.

3. Cover the dish with foil. Cook the chicken in the oven for about 40 minutes, then carefully lift out the dish.

4. To see if the chicken is cooked, push a skewer into it. If pink juice runs out, you need to cook it for longer.

Kebabs

Ingredients

For the marinade:
- the juice of a lemon
- 6 Tablespoons cooking oil
- a pinch of your choice of seasonings
- salt and black pepper

- 1 lb. boned lamb or beef
- 8 small mushrooms
- 1 large onion
- 4 tomatoes

You will also need metal skewers.

The meat used in these kebabs is soaked in a sauce called a marinade, which makes it tender. Soak it for a few hours, if you can.

1. Mix the lemon juice, oil, seasonings and a pinch of salt and pepper in a bowl. Cut the meat into cubes, then mix it in.

2. Wipe the mushrooms. Peel the onion, cut it into quarters and separate the layers. Then, cut the tomatoes into quarters.

3. Lift the meat out of the marinade. Push everything tightly onto the metal skewers, watching out for the sharp ends.

4. Wearing oven mitts, put the kebabs on the grill or broiler. Cook them for about 10-15 minutes, carefully turning them every few minutes. They are cooked when the meat is brown on the outside but still juicy in the middle. Serve them with rice (see page 30) and a salad.

Pizza

Ingredients

- ½ cup warm water
- 1 teaspoon sugar
- 1 teaspoon rapid-rise yeast
- 1¾ cups white bread flour
- ½ teaspoon salt
- 16 oz. can tomatoes
- 1 Tablespoon tomato paste
- salt and black pepper
- 1¼ cups grated cheese
- 1 teaspoon dried oregano

Bread dough takes a long time to rise, so you'll need to start making it about 2½ hours before you want to eat your pizzas.

Preheat your oven to 400°F.
Grease two 8 inch round pizza trays, too.

1. Following the directions on the yeast package, add the water, yeast and sugar to a container.

2. Sift the flour and salt into a bowl, then mix in the yeast. Mix in just enough of the water to make a soft ball of dough that leaves the bowl clean.

4. Cover the bowl with plastic foodwrap. Put it in a warm place for about an hour, to rise.

3. Dust flour over a clean work surface. Put the dough onto the floured surface and knead it for about five minutes (see page 71). When the dough is smooth and stretchy, put it into a greased bowl.

5. When the dough has doubled in size, take it out of the bowl. Knead it for five more minutes.

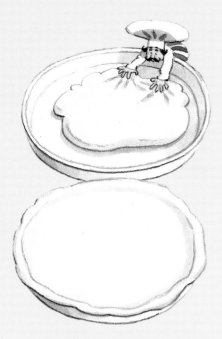

6. Break the dough into two balls and put one in each pan. Press them with your fingers until they fill the pans, then pinch the edges to make crusts.

7. Drain the tomatoes using a sieve. Then, put the sieve over a bowl and push the tomato through it with a wooden spoon. Stir in the tomato paste and a pinch of salt and pepper.

8. Spread the tomato sauce over the pizzas, but don't spread it on the crusts. Sprinkle the cheese and seasoning over the sauce.

9. Bake the pizzas on the middle shelf of the oven for 20 minutes, until the crusts are crisp and brown.

10. Carefully lift out the pizzas. Cut them into wedges, then eat them right away. You could vary the pizza topping by adding things like sliced mushrooms or peppers, olives, anchovies, pepperoni or strips of Canadian bacon in step 8.

Mixed Salad

Ingredients

- ½ crisp lettuce
- ¼ cucumber
- 2 tomatoes
- 2 sticks celery
- 2 carrots
- 1 eating apple

Basic Dressing

- 3 Tablespoons cooking oil
- 1 Tablespoon vinegar
- a pinch of mustard powder
- a pinch of salt and black pepper
- a pinch of sugar

Put all of the ingredients into a glass jar with a lid. Screw the lid on tightly, then shake the jar well.

1. Break the lettuce leaves into pieces. Cut the cucumber into thick slices, then cut the slices into chunks.

2. Cut the tomatoes and celery into chunks. Peel the carrots and core the apple. Then, cut them up.

Don't add the dressing any earlier, or it will make the salad soggy.

3. Mix all the ingredients in a large bowl. Just before you serve the salad, pour on the dressing and mix it in.

Potato Salad

Ingredients

- 1 lb. small, white potatoes, scrubbed clean
- three green onions
- 4 Tablespoons salad dressing (see box on page 36)
- salt and black pepper
- 1 Tablespoon chopped parsley

1. Cook the potatoes in boiling water for 15-20 minutes, or until they are tender.

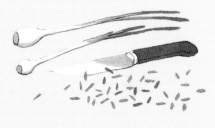

2. Drain the potatoes well, using a colander.

3. Trim off the ends and outer layer of the green onions. Chop them finely.

4. Leave the potatoes to cool. Then, cut them in half or into quarters with a sharp knife.

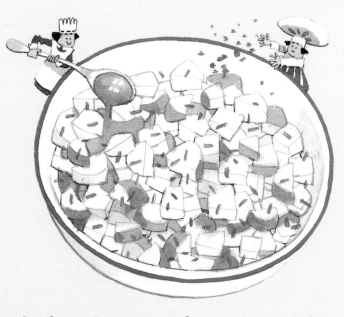

5. Put the chopped potatoes and green onions into a large bowl. Pour the dressing over the top and add a pinch of salt and pepper. Mix the salad gently, then sprinkle the chopped parsley over the top.

Apple Crumble

Ingredients

- 2 lbs. cooking apples
- ¼ cup soft brown sugar
- 2 Tablespoons orange juice
- ½ teaspoon ground cinnamon

For the crumble topping:
- 1½ cups all-purpose flour
- a pinch of salt
- 6 Tablespoons butter
- ¼ cup sugar

Preheat your oven to 400°F.

You can make a crumble with any fruit you like — try plums, raspberries or blackberries.

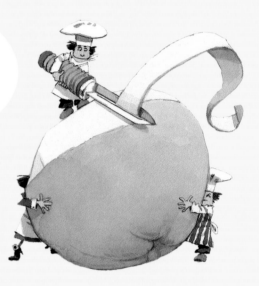

1. Carefully peel the apples with a potato peeler.

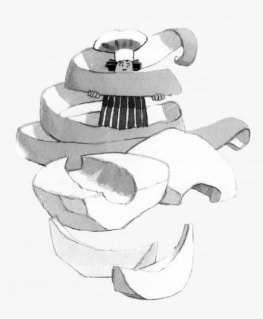

2. Cut the apples in half and cut out the cores. Slice the apples.

3. Put the apples, brown sugar, orange juice and cinnamon into a saucepan. Cook them over low heat until the apples are soft.

4. Spoon the apples into a 1 quart casserole dish and spread them out evenly.

5. Sift the flour and salt into a large bowl. Cut the butter into small pieces and add it to the bowl.

6. Rub the butter into the flour with the tips of your fingers. Lift your hands and let the pieces fall into the bowl. This makes the mixture light. Continue until you have a crumbly mixture that looks like breadcrumbs, then stir in the sugar.

7. Spoon the crumble mixture over the apples. Spread it out with a fork, but don't press it down.

8. Bake the crumble for about 25-30 minutes, or until the top is golden brown. Check it while it is cooking. Serve it with ice cream.

Fresh Fruit Salad

Ingredients

- 1 orange
- ½ lemon
- 1 pear
- 2 bananas
- 2 peaches
- 1 cup strawberries
- ½ cup raspberries
- sugar

You can mix any fruit you like into your fruit salad.

1. Squeeze the juice from the orange and lemon using a lemon squeezer. Then, pour the juice into a large bowl.

2. Peel the pear, then cut its core. Slice the pear and put the slices into the bowl. Peel the banana and slice it, then add it to the bowl, too. Gently stir the fruit into the juice, to keep it from turning brown.

4. Carefully cut the peaches in half, then remove the pits with a teaspoon.

5. Peel the peaches, then slice them. Rinse the strawberries and raspberries, then pat them dry with paper towels. Then, cut the stalks out of the strawberries and cut any big strawberries into quarters.

You could include any of these fruits in a fruit salad: apples, oranges, grapes, plums, cherries, apricots or pineapples.

6. Add the peaches, strawberries and raspberries to the fruit in the bowl. Sprinkle a little sugar over the fruit and gently mix everything together. Put the fruit salad in the refrigerator to chill for at least an hour.

Juicy Oranges

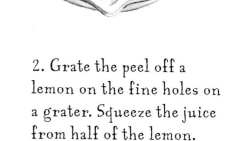

Ingredients

- 6 oranges
- 1 lemon
- 2 Tablespoons sugar

1. Carefully peel four oranges, then cut off the white pith. Slice them and take out any seeds.

2. Grate the peel off a lemon on the fine holes on a grater. Squeeze the juice from half of the lemon.

You could eat the oranges with whipped cream or ice cream.

3. Put the slices of orange into a dish. Sprinkle the sugar and grated lemon peel over them. Then, squeeze the juice from the other two oranges.

4. Pour the juice over the sliced oranges. Gently mix everything together, then put the oranges in the refrigerator to chill.

Pear Flan

Ingredients

- ½ cup butter
- 3 eggs
- ½ cup sugar
- 1 cup all-purpose flour
- a few drops vanilla
- a pinch of salt
- 5 pears

Preheat your oven to 350°F. Grease an ovenproof flan dish, too.

1. Put the butter into a saucepan and heat it over low heat until it melts.

2. Beat the eggs and sugar together. Stir in the butter, then stir in the flour, a little at a time. Mix in the vanilla and the pinch of salt, too.

3. Peel the skin off the pears, then cut them into quarters. Carefully cut out the cores and seeds from each piece.

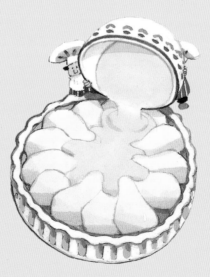

4. Pour some of the eggy mixture into the dish. Lay the pears on top, then pour in the rest of the mixture.

5. Bake the flan in the oven for about 45 minutes until it is golden brown.

Lemon Cheesecake

Ingredients

- about 24 ginger snap cookies
- 4 Tablespoons butter
- 1 lemon
- 8 oz. cream cheese
- 1 can sweetened condensed milk
- 1 Tablespoon sugar
- grated chocolate or lemon peel, for decorating

Grease an 8 inch round flan or pie dish, before you start.

1. Break the cookies into a plastic bag. Then, roll a rolling pin over them, to crush them into fine crumbs.

2. Melt the butter in a saucepan over low heat. Add the cookie crumbs and stir them in well.

3. Press the mixture evenly into the flan or pie dish with a spoon. Then, put it in the refrigerator to harden.

4. Grate the lemon rind on the fine holes on a grater. Cut the lemon in half, then squeeze out the juice using a lemon squeezer.

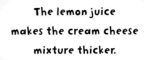

The lemon juice makes the cream cheese mixture thicker.

5. Put the cream cheese into a large bowl and beat it with a wooden spoon until it is soft. Add the condensed milk a little at a time, beating the mixture all the time. Continue until the mixture is smooth.

6. Quickly stir the sugar, lemon rind and juice into the cream cheese mixture.

7. When the mixture is smooth, pour it over the cookie base. Flatten the top with a knife.

8. Cover the cheesecake with foil and put it in the refrigerator to chill for at least three hours. When the middle has set, sprinkle grated chocolate or lemon peel over the top of the cheesecake.

Crêpes

Ingredients

- 2 cups all-purpose flour
- a pinch of salt
- 2 eggs
- 2½ cups milk and water mixed together
- 1 Tablespoon melted butter
- sunflower oil

1. Sift the flour and salt into a large mixing bowl. Make a hollow in the middle of the mixture with a spoon.

2. Break the eggs and pour them into the hollow in the flour. Then, gently whisk them, drawing in some flour from the sides.

You can put the batter aside until you are ready to use it, but you'll need to stir it well before you make your crêpes.

3. Add the milk and water mixture, a little at time. Continue whisking and drawing in the flour until everything is mixed together.

4. Add a Tablespoon of melted butter. Then, beat the mixture until you make a smooth batter that is just thick enough to coat a wooden spoon.

5. Heat a small frying pan over a medium flame for no more than a minute, then wipe some oil over the bottom of the pan. Then, pour in half a cup of batter.

6. Quickly and carefully tilt the pan in all directions until a thin layer of batter covers the bottom.

7. Cook the crêpe until bubbles appear and the edges begin to turn brown. Turn the crêpe over with a spatula, then cook the other side.

8. Slide the crêpe out of the pan onto a warm plate. You could sprinkle it with lemon juice and sugar, and roll it up. Then, make another one.

9. Eat the crêpes right away, while they are hot. You could spread them with warm jam, honey or chocolate sauce, instead of lemon juice and sugar.

Cream Puffs

Ingredients

- 4 Tablespoons butter
- ⅔ cup water
- ½ cup all-purpose flour
- 2 eggs, lightly beaten
- a small carton of whipping cream and ¼ cup powdered sugar

For the sauce:
- ½ cup chocolate chips
- 2 Tablespoons water

Cream puffs are light, puffy little buns made of 'choux' pastry. You make the pastry in a saucepan.

Preheat your oven to 400°F.

1. Grease two baking sheets, then hold them under cold running water for a few seconds.

2. Cut the butter into small pieces. Heat it in a saucepan with the water over low heat. Sift the flour onto a sheet of greaseproof paper.

3. When the mixture in the pan starts to boil, take it off the heat and pour in all the flour.

4. Beat the mixture for a minute, until it is smooth and comes away from the sides of the pan easily.

5. Let the mixture cool for about five minutes. Then, add a little egg and stir it in hard. Repeat this until you've added all the egg.

6. Put teaspoons of the mixture onto the baking sheets and put them in the oven. After 10 minutes, raise the temperature to 425°F.

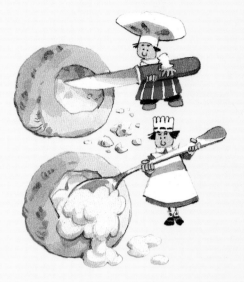

7. Bake the puffs for another 10-15 minutes, until they are golden brown and puffy. Then, lift them out of the oven.

8. Put the puffs on a wire rack to cool. Cut a hole in the side of each one with the point of a knife, to let out any steam.

9. Whisk the cream and sugar until it is thick and forms peaks when you lift the whisk. Then, use a teaspoon to fill the hollow inside each cream puff with cream.

10. To make the sauce, put the chocolate and water into a heatproof bowl. Heat it gently over a pan of bubbling water until the chocolate melts. Stir the sauce until it's smooth.

11. Pile the cream puffs in a heap on a large plate, then pour the hot chocolate sauce over them. Serve them right away, while the sauce is still hot.

Strawberry Tarts

Ingredients

- 1½ cups all-purpose flour
- 6 Tablespoons butter
- 6 Tablespoons sugar
- a pinch of salt
- 3 egg yolks, beaten
- 1 lb. strawberries
- 6 oz. strawberry jelly

Preheat your oven to 400°F.

1. Sift the flour into a bowl and rub it in with the butter, sugar and salt, to make a crumbly mixture (see page 39).

2. Add the egg yolks and mix them in well with a knife. Squeeze the mixture with your hands, to make a smooth ball of dough.

The dough should be soft but not sticky. Add a little water if it is dry, or a little more flour if it is sticky. To make it easier to roll out, put it in the refrigerator for 30 minutes.

3. Roll out the dough until it is fairly thin. Cut out four circles of dough with a round cutter. Press them into little metal flan tins.

4. Prick the pastry cases with a fork, then line them with greaseproof paper. Lay dried beans on top of the paper, to keep the pastry from puffing up.

5. Bake the pastry cases for 15 minutes, then take out the paper and beans. Bake the cases for five more minutes, until they are light brown, then cool them on a wire rack.

6. Wash the strawberries and take out the stalks. Cut any big strawberries in half.

7. Melt the strawberry jelly in a small pan over low heat, to make a glaze. Then, take it off the heat.

8. When the pastry cases are cool, brush the insides with a thick coat of the strawberry glaze. Arrange the strawberries in the cases and brush them with more of the glaze. Leave the glaze to cool, so that it sets.

Other Fruit Tarts

You can fill pastry cases with grapes, raspberries, blueberries or apricots, too.

Ice Cream Sundaes

Making ice cream sundaes is really fun. To make some, you'll need several different flavors of ice cream, yummy sauces (see opposite), fruit and grated chocolate. Here are some ideas you could try:

mixed ice cream with chocolate sauce

caramel ice cream with toffee sauce

vanilla ice cream, sliced banana and raspberry sauce

vanilla ice cream, pears and chocolate sauce

Chocolate Sauce

- ½ cup semi-sweet chocolate
- 3 Tablespoons water

1. Break the chocolate into pieces. Then, put the pieces into a heatproof bowl and add the water.

2. Carefully place the bowl into a saucepan of gently bubbling water. Stir the sauce as the chocolate melts.

Raspberry Sauce

- 8 oz. raspberries
- 4 Tablespoons sugar

1. Wash the raspberries, then press them through a sieve into a bowl.

2. Stir in one teaspoonful of sugar at a time. Stir it in well, until it dissolves.

Toffee Sauce

- 2 Tablespoons butter or margarine
- ⅓ cup brown sugar
- 2 Tablespoons corn syrup
- 4 Tablespoons cream

1. Melt the butter, sugar and syrup in a saucepan over low heat. Don't let the mixture boil.

2. Add the cream and stir it in. You can serve the sauce hot or cold.

Granola

Eat granola for breakfast. It will give you lots of energy.

Ingredients

- 1 cup oatmeal
- 1 Tablespoon wheatgerm
- ⅓ cup raisins
- ½ cup chopped nuts*
- 2 apples
- 8 oz. carton of plain yogurt
- milk
- honey or brown sugar

1. Mix the oatmeal, wheatgerm, raisins and nuts in a large bowl. Peel the apples and cut out the cores, then grate them. Quickly stir them into the granola, so that they don't turn brown, then add the yogurt.

You can make lots of granola and keep it in a storage jar. Spoon it into bowls and add the apple and yogurt when you're ready to eat it.

2. Pour milk over the granola, then add a little honey or brown sugar.

3. You could add a sliced banana, strawberries or slices of peach, too.

54   * Don't give the granola to anyone who is allergic to nuts.

Banana And Honey Whip

Ingredients

- 8 oz. carton of whipping cream
- 4 ripe bananas
- 1½ small 8 oz. cartons of plain yogurt
- 2 Tablespoons honey
- 1 Tablespoon lemon juice
- a handful of flaked almonds*

1. Beat the cream in a bowl with a whisk until it is fluffy and forms peaks when you lift the whisk.

2. Peel the bananas and slice them. Mash them in another bowl with a fork.

Sprinkle the flaked almonds over the top.

3. Add the yogurt, honey and lemon juice to the mashed banana, then stir them in.

4. Add the whipped cream and fold it in. Then, spoon the whip into serving dishes.

* Don't give the banana and honey whip to anyone who is allergic to nuts.

Oatmeal Squares

Ingredients

- ½ cup butter
- ¾ cup brown sugar
- 2 Tablespoons corn syrup
- 2½ cups oatmeal
- ½ cup raisins

Preheat your oven to 325°F.

Grease a shallow 7 x 11 inch rectangular pan.

1. Put the butter, sugar and syrup in a saucepan. Melt them over very low heat and carefully stir them with a wooden spoon.

2. Take the pan off the heat. Add the oatmeal and raisins to the mixture and stir everything well.

3. Pour the mixture into the pan and press it down. Then, bake it for 20-25 minutes.

4. Lift out the pan, then carefully cut the mixture into squares. Leave them to cool, then lift them out of the pan. Store them in an airtight container.

Chocolate Brownies

Ingredients

- ½ cup semi-sweet chocolate
- 10 Tablespoons butter
- 1¼ cups sugar
- 2 eggs, beaten
- ¼ cup all-purpose flour
- 2 Tablespoons cocoa powder
- ½ cup chopped walnuts*
- a pinch of salt
- ½ teaspoon vanilla

Preheat your oven to 350°F.
Grease a shallow 7 x 11 inch rectangular pan, too.

1. Break the chocolate into a heatproof bowl. Add the butter. Carefully put the bowl into a saucepan of gently bubbling water.

2. When the butter and chocolate have melted, take the bowl off the heat. Then, stir in all the other ingredients.

The brownies will be crisp on the top and gooey in the middle.

3. Pour the mixture into the pan and spread it out. Bake it in the oven for 30-35 minutes.

4. Lift out the pan and leave the brownies in it for 10 minutes. Then, cut them into squares and put them onto a wire rack to cool completely. Store them in an airtight container.

* Don't give the chocolate brownies to anyone who is allergic to nuts.

Marmalade Gingerbread

Ingredients

- 6 Tablespoons butter or margarine
- ½ cup corn syrup
- 1 cup self-rising flour
- 2 teaspoons ground ginger
- 1 teaspoon ground cinnamon
- a pinch of salt
- 1 cup (8 oz.) chunky marmalade
- 1 egg, beaten
- 1 Tablespoon hot water

Before you start, grease a 7 inch square cake pan and line it with baking parchment, like this:

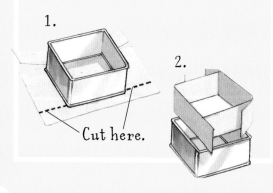

Cut here.

Preheat your oven to 325°F.

1. Cut up the butter, then melt it with the syrup in a saucepan over low heat. Take the pan off the heat.

2. Sift the flour, ginger, cinnamon and salt into a bowl. Make a hollow in the middle with a spoon.

3. Slowly pour the syrup mixture into the hollow, stirring in the flour from the sides as you do so. Add the marmalade, egg and water and mix everything well.

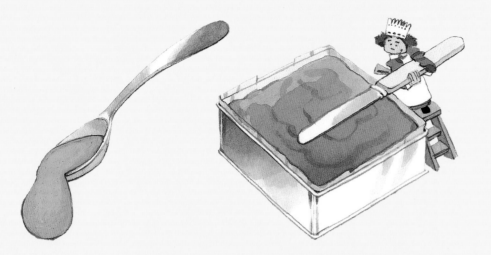

4. The mixture should be soft and should slide off a spoon easily. If it is too thick, add a little more water.

5. Pour the mixture into the cake pan. Spread it out evenly with a knife.

6. Put the pan into the oven and bake the gingerbread for an hour.

7. Carefully lift the pan out of the oven. It should be golden brown and feel springy in the middle. If you push a skewer into the middle of the cake, it should come out clean, too.

8. Leave the cake to cool in the pan for 15 minutes. Then, turn it out onto a wire rack to cool.

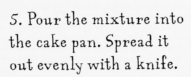

Store the cake in an airtight container, or a covered cake pan.

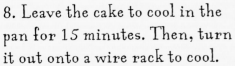

Fudge

Grease a 6 x 6 inch baking pan, before you start.

Be very careful not to let the mixture boil over!

Ingredients

- 3 cups brown sugar
- 3 Tablespoons butter or margarine
- 1 Tablespoon light corn syrup
- 1 cup evaporated milk
- 1 teaspoon vanilla

BE CAREFUL

Boiling sugar can be dangerous. Don't make fudge unless an adult is there to help you.

1. Heat the sugar, butter, corn syrup and milk in a saucepan, until the sugar melts. Stirring the mixture all the time, bring it to a boil. Boil it for 30 minutes.

2. Drop a little fudge into a bowl of cold water. It should form a soft ball. If not, keep boiling and testing it until it does.

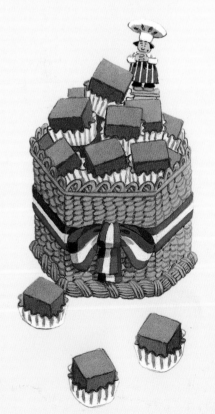

3. Take the pan off the heat. Add the vanilla, then beat it in, until the mixture is thick and creamy. Pour the mixture into the pan.

4. Leave the fudge to set. Then, carefully cut it into squares with a sharp knife.

Meringues

Preheat your oven to 225°F.

Ingredients

- 4 egg whites
  (Follow steps 1-2 on page 23 to separate the egg whites from the yolks. If you like, you could use the yolks to make the strawberry tarts on pages 50-51.)
- 7 Tablespoons sugar

Use an electric mixer, if you have one.

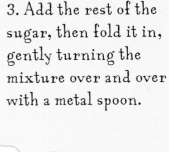

1. Wipe two baking trays with cooking oil, then sift a little flour over the top. Tap the sides of the trays, to spread out the flour.

2. Whisk the egg whites in a big bowl until they are stiff. Then, add half of the sugar, a teaspoonful at a time. Whisk the mixture all the time.

3. Add the rest of the sugar, then fold it in, gently turning the mixture over and over with a metal spoon.

4. Drop Tablespoonfuls of the mixture onto the baking sheets, 1 inch apart. Shape them into circles.

5. Bake the meringues for 40 minutes. Then, turn off the oven, leaving them inside for 15 minutes.

6. Eat your meringues plain, or stick pairs of them together with whipped cream.

Fruit Cake

Ingredients

- 3 medium eggs
- ⅓ cup candied cherries
- ¾ cup butter
- ¾ cup soft brown sugar
- 1 teaspoon baking powder
- 2 cups all-purpose flour
- ⅔ cup raisins
- ⅔ cup seedless white raisins
- ⅓ cup candied peel
- a pinch of salt
- 1 teaspoon all-spice
- ⅓ cup ground almonds*
- ⅓ cup almonds*

Preheat your oven to 275°F. Grease the inside of a 7-8 inch round cake pan with butter, too.

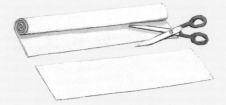 

1. Cut a strip of baking parchment or greaseproof paper that is long enough to go around the cake pan.

2. Fold back ¾ inch along one edge, then snip cuts into it, like this.

 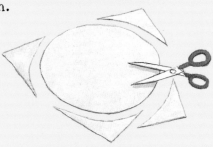

3. Line the inside of the pan with the paper strip.

4. Cut a circle of paper to line the bottom of the pan.

You'll find it easier to make the cake if you take the butter and eggs out of the refrigerator an hour before you start.

5. Beat the eggs. Rinse and dry the cherries and cut them in half.

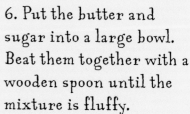

6. Put the butter and sugar into a large bowl. Beat them together with a wooden spoon until the mixture is fluffy.

* Don't give this cake to anyone who is allergic to nuts.

7. Mix in the eggs, a little at a time. Gently fold in the baking powder and flour. The mixture should drop off a spoon easily.

8. If the mixture is too thick, stir in a little milk. Add the dried fruit, then carefully fold it in, using a large spoon (see page 71). Gently fold in the cherries, salt, candied peel, all-spice and ground almonds, too.

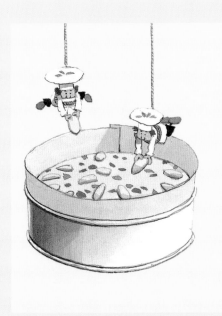

9. Spoon the mixture into the pan and smooth out the top. Gently arrange the almonds on top of the cake.

10. Bake the cake for 2-2½ hours. It is cooked when the middle feels springy. If you push a skewer into the cake, it should come out clean, too. When the cake is cool, turn it out of the pan. Store it in an airtight container.

Iced Spice Cookies

Ingredients

- ½ cup butter
- ½ cup brown sugar
- 1 small egg, beaten
- 2 cups all-purpose flour
- a pinch of salt
- 2 teaspoons all-spice

For the icing:
- ½ cup powdered sugar
- 1-2 Tablespoons warm water
- food colorings

Preheat your oven to 375°F. Grease two baking trays, too.

1. Beat the butter and sugar together until they are fluffy. Then, beat in the egg, a little at a time.

2. Sift the flour, salt and all-spice into the bowl. Mix everything well, to make a ball of firm dough.

3. Sprinkle flour onto a clean work surface and a rolling pin. Then, roll out the dough until it is about ¼ inch thick.

4. Using cutters, cut shapes from the dough. Squeeze any scraps into a ball, roll it out and cut out more shapes.

5. Put the shapes onto the baking trays. Bake them in the oven for 12-15 minutes, until they are pale brown.

6. Lift the cookies onto a wire rack to cool. Then, sift the powdered sugar into a bowl and mix in the warm water, until the icing is smooth.

7. Spoon the icing into three cups. Put one cup to one side, then mix a few drops of food coloring into the other two cups.

8. When the cookies are completely cool, spoon a teaspoon of icing onto each one and spread it out with a knife.

9. Before the icing sets, press little candies onto the cookies. Then, leave the icing to set.

Sticky Chocolate Cake

Ingredients

- 1 cup semi-sweet chocolate
- ¾ cup butter, softened
- ¾ cup sugar
- 4 eggs, separated into whites and yolks (see page 23)
- ¾ cup ground almonds
- ¾ cup all-purpose flour

For the sticky chocolate icing:
- ⅓ cup evaporated milk
- 6 Tablespoons sugar
- ⅔ cup (4 oz.) semi-sweet chocolate
- 3 Tablespoons butter or margarine

3. Whisk the egg whites in a big bowl until they form soft peaks when you lift the whisk.

Preheat your oven to 350°F. Grease two 8 inch round cake pans, too.

1. Break the chocolate into a bowl. Carefully put it into a pan of gently bubbling water, then stir the chocolate as it melts.

2. Cream the butter and sugar until they are fluffy. Beat the egg yolks, then add them a little at a time. Stir in the melted chocolate and almonds.

Fold in the egg white gently.

4. Add some egg white to the mixture. Gently fold it in, then fold in some flour. Continue until you have used them both up.

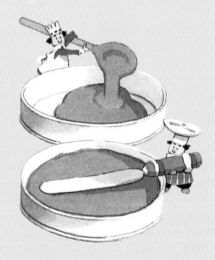

5. Pour the mixture into the pans and spread it out. Bake the cakes for 20 minutes, until their middles feel springy.

6. While the cake is baking, make the icing. Heat the evaporated milk and sugar over low heat, stirring all the time. Bring the sauce to a boil, then let it simmer for five minutes.

7. Take the pan off the heat. Break the chocolate into the pan and stir it until it melts. Then, stir in the butter until it melts.

8. Pour the icing into a bowl. When it is cool, put it in the refrigerator. As it cools, it thickens and becomes easier to spread.

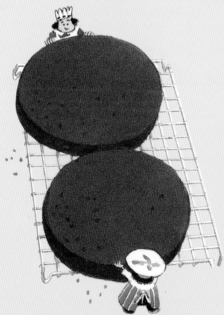

9. Leave the cakes in the pans for a few minutes, then run a knife around the sides. Turn the cakes out onto a wire rack to cool.

10. When the cake and icing are cool, spread half of the icing on top of the cake. Lay the other cake on top and spread it with the rest of the icing.

Handy Hints

Mixing

Use a wooden spoon when you're mixing ingredients together, stirring things in a saucepan or adding eggs or egg yolks to a mixture.

Beating Eggs

Beat eggs with a whisk or fork until they are mixed and frothy. Stand the bowl on a damp cloth to keep it from sliding around.

Whisking Eggs

Use an electric mixer, if you have one.

Whisk egg whites until they become stiff and you get points or 'peaks' on the top when you lift up the whisk.

Greasing A Pan

Wipe a paper towel in a little butter or margarine. Rub the paper towel around the inside of the pan until it is lightly greased all over.

Icing A Cake

To spread icing easily, dip a blunt knife into warm water and use it to smooth the icing over the top and sides of the cake.

Looking Good

If you want to decorate a cake or dessert before you serve it, you could arrange twists of lemon or orange on the top.

Preparing Vegetables

1. Wash vegetables well in cold water, but don't soak them for too long. If they're gritty, scrub them clean with a brush that is only used for food.

2. Peel any carrots and big potatoes. Little 'new' potatoes just need to be washed or gently scraped clean with a knife.

3. Cut any wilted leaves, tough stalks, tops or roots off green vegetables. Then, slice or chop them into pieces.

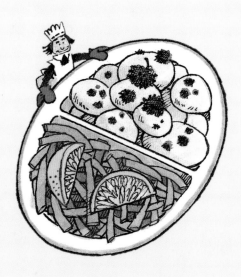

4. Half-fill a saucepan with water. Add a pinch of salt, then boil the water. Cook the vegetables with the lid on, then push a skewer into them to see if they're cooked.

5. If the vegetables are tender, but still a little crunchy, they are cooked. Carefully pour them into a colander in the sink, to drain them.

6. Serve the vegetables right away. You could decorate them with sprigs of parsley, pieces of chopped parsley or slices of lemon.

Kitchen Equipment

frying pan

saucepan

wire rack

rolling pin

cutting board

large mixing bowl

measuring cup

colander

cake pan

flan pan

sieve

timer

potato peeler

whisks (egg beater, wire whisk)

spatula

ovenproof casserole dish

pastry brush

baking tray

pepper grinder

palette knife

can opener

lemon squeezer

garlic press

cookie cutters

rubber spatula

grater

kitchen scissors

kitchen scales*

kitchen knives

* Scales are used in some countries to weigh dry ingredients.

Cooking Words

BAKE — Cook in an oven.

BEAT — Mix by stirring vigorously with a fork, a wooden spoon or a whisk.

BOIL — Cook in boiling water.

BRING TO A BOIL — Heat a liquid until it starts to bubble.

BROIL — Cook food in a broiler.

CREAM — Beat butter and sugar together with a wooden spoon.

FOLD IN — Gently mix an ingredient into a creamed mixture, using a metal spoon.

FRY — Cook in hot fat or oil.

GARNISH — Decorate food with things such as chopped parsley.

GLAZE — Coat food with beaten egg, milk or melted fruit preserves, to make it look shiny.

GREASE — Rub the inside of a baking pan or ovenproof dish with butter or margarine, to keep food from sticking to it.

KNEAD — Work a dough firmly with your hands by pushing it away from you, then folding it in half and pushing it again and again until it's smooth and stretchy.

MARINADE — A mixture in which you soak meat or fish before cooking it, to make it tender and to give it flavor.

RUB IN — Rub fat into flour with your fingertips until the mixture looks like breadcrumbs.

SEPARATE AN EGG — To divide the egg white from the yolk.

SIFT — Shake flour or powdered sugar through a sieve, to get rid of lumps and make it light.

SIMMER — Cook a liquid over low heat so that it is just bubbling, but not boiling.

WHISK — Beat vigorously with a whisk, egg beater or electric mixer, to add air to a mixture and make it light.

Index

Digital manipulation by Isaac Quaye • With thanks to Samantha Meredith